THE X-TAILS
BMX AT
THUNDER TRACK

WRITTEN BY L.A. Fielding

ILLUSTRATED BY Victor Guiza

Library and Archives Canada Cataloguing in Publication

Fielding, L. A. (Lawrence Anthony), 1977-, author
BMX at Thunder Track / author: L.A. Fielding ; illustrator: Victor Guiza.

(The X-tails)
Issued in print and electronic formats.
ISBN 978-1-928199-00-7 (pbk.).

I. Guiza, Victor, illustrator II. Title. III. Series: Fielding, L. A. (Lawrence Anthony), 1977- X-tails

PS8611.I362B59 2015   jC813'.6   C2015-900730-5   C2015-900731-3

Copyright © 2015 The X-tails Enterprises

The X-tails Enterprises
Prince George, BC Canada

Printed in Canada

Design and text layout by Margaret Cogswell
www.spiderbuddydesigns.com

To Cru Jones and Bart Taylor.
Thanks for being zoober-Rad!

MEET THE X-TAILS!

WISDOM

The smart and responsible lion who is the natural leader of the X-tails. He is a master at solving problems and can fix almost anything. Wisdom loves to **"ROOaaaRRRR!"** when he is having fun.

CHARM

The cute and bubbly kangaroo. She loves the spotlight and performing at contests in front of big crowds. Her kangaroo legs are perfect for jumping high and pedaling fast. When Charm is really happy, you will see her **HOP** around or **THUMP** her foot with a big smile.

CRASH

The clumsy, messy, and very goofy hippo. Crash usually finds himself in all sorts of trouble and is thankful that his X-tail friends are always there when he needs them. You can't help but laugh with Crash at the many silly things he does, especially when he bellows **"GaaaWHOOOOMPHaaaaa!"**

FLIGHT

The strong and fearless rocker gorilla. Flight not only plays the air guitar but also loves to play on any jump he can find. Although he is really big and hairy, this gorilla is a gentle giant. You know Flight is ready for air time when you hear him grunt **"OOOHHHH, OOOHHHH, OOOHHHH!"**

Dazzle

The tough and brave bear who is a tomboy at heart. The boys have difficulty keeping up with Dazzle. And good luck trying to slow her down! She has a big grin, and you will often hear her friendly growl, **"GRRRRR!"**

MISCHIEF

The practical joker of the bunch. You know Mischief is up to something sneaky when you see his mischievous grin. He is a little short for a wolf, so be careful you don't confuse him with a fox—he doesn't like that much. But being small always works to his advantage. You will hear Mischief howl **"aaaaWHOOOOO!"** when he is excited.

And we can't forget about the X-van, which takes the X-tails to the mountains, ocean, BMX tracks, and skateboard parks. This off-road machine can go anywhere and easily fits all of the X-tails' gear. Wisdom the Lion is always the driver of the X-van.

THE X-Van

CLANG ... CLATTER ...
smash!

Charm the Kangaroo tumbled head over tail in the dirt.
Her BMX bike lay on the ground in pieces.

In a flash, the X-tails pedaled their bikes over to Charm.

"What a wipe out! Are you okay?" asked Flight the Gorilla.

"I think so, but my bike is a wreck," said Charm. As he helped her up, she suddenly shrieked!

"**OWWWW,** my arm!"

"Oh oh," said Flight. "Let's get you to the doctor right away!"

At the doctor's office, Charm was in the examining room for a long time. Finally, the door opened and she slowly walked out. She was hiding something behind her back.

"What's wrong?" asked Dazzle the Bear.

"It's the worst news ever," said Charm. "I'm not allowed to bike for a whole month!" Wiping away the tears, she showed them her arm—it was in a cast!

The X-tails knew why she was so sad—the Thunder Track BMX race was only a month away. There was no other race like it, and best of all, it was the chance to win the

GOLDEN BIKE!

With a broken arm, Charm's dream of racing at Thunder Track seemed impossible.

Back at home, the X-tails wrote on Charm's cast to make her feel better. Then they headed out the door to practice for the race. Charm stared sadly out her bedroom window, wishing she could bike with her friends.

As the weeks went by, Charm no longer smiled.
The Thunder Track race was now only two days away
and Wisdom the Lion had an idea to cheer her up.

When everyone went to bed, he snuck out to the
garage on a top secret mission. He worked all night
tinkering with tools, and by morning was ready to
surprise Charm with a present.

Tiptoeing like a ninja, Wisdom placed the gift outside her bedroom door. He knocked loudly before hiding behind the couch. Charm opened the door, but no one was there. Then she saw it!

"SURPRISE!"

yelled Wisdom.

The room instantly grew brighter—Charm was smiling! Hopping around the house, she shouted, "Thank you … thank you … thank you!"

Soon the noise woke all of the X-tails.

 growled Dazzle.

"Your bike is zoober-sweet! To top it off, you get your cast off today. Now you can race at Thunder Track tomorrow!"

Charm stopped hopping and her smile disappeared. "I can't race at Thunder Track. I haven't been practicing. I can't do it!"

Wisdom couldn't believe his ears. "Can't . . . can't. Yes, you can!" he said. "As long as the doctor says your arm is okay, you can race at Thunder Track. You just have to try!"

Unsure if her friend was right, Charm
left the house to get her cast off.

The next day, the X-tails buzzed excitedly when they arrived at Thunder Track.

"Look!" said Mischief the Wolf. "We have to jump over ooey-gooey slime!"

"Hey, over there!" pointed Flight. "We have to ride across an airplane!"

"And I see a loop de loop! We get to go upside down!" shouted Wisdom.

Everyone was excited except for Charm. The doctor had said she could race, but Thunder Track looked scary! Remembering what Wisdom had told her, she whispered to herself, "I can do it. I can do it!"

Feeling better, she joined her friends for their safety check. Wearing helmets, gloves, race pants and jerseys, they were ready for fur-blowing speed!

The rules were simple. Four animals raced in each qualifying race. The first animal across the finish line would be in the final race.

START

Mischief the Wolf and Crash the Hippo lined up beside a jumpy giraffe and a radical rhino. The horn blasted and they pedaled hard out of the start gate!

"GaaaWHOOOOMPHaaaaa!"

bellowed Crash as he clumsily took the lead. Right behind him was Mischief, who had a plan.

Crash grinned, thinking he was going to win, but his legs felt tired. The track was sooo long. He began to breathe harder and harder.

Just before the finish line, Mischief put his plan into action. Because he had saved his energy, he was able to pedal zoober-fast. He passed Crash and finished first! The crowd howled in delight, so naturally, Mischief howled back.

Things didn't go well for some of the X-tails and they had wild wipe outs. Dazzle got slimed.

Flight missed his plane ride.

And Wisdom got a flat tire and only made it halfway around the loop de loop. Luckily, he landed on the safety mattress.

Now it was Charm's turn for her qualifying race.
Lining up, she looked over her shoulder and saw...

a moustached moose,

a toothy tiger,

and a peachy pig.

The horn sounded and they bolted out of the start
gate. Charm stayed at the back of the pack. After
landing a few jumps, she was no longer worried.
Her bike felt zoober-awesome!

She jumped over the pig, who had decided to take a bath in the slime.

Next up was the plane— no problem!

Then Charm waved bye-bye to the moose as she rocketed around the loop de loop!

Charm was in second place and right behind the toothy tiger. She saw the finish line coming, so she made her move. Darting low, she kicked her kangaroo legs into high gear to cross the finish line first!

The crowd went bonkers! Charm had made it to the FINAL race!

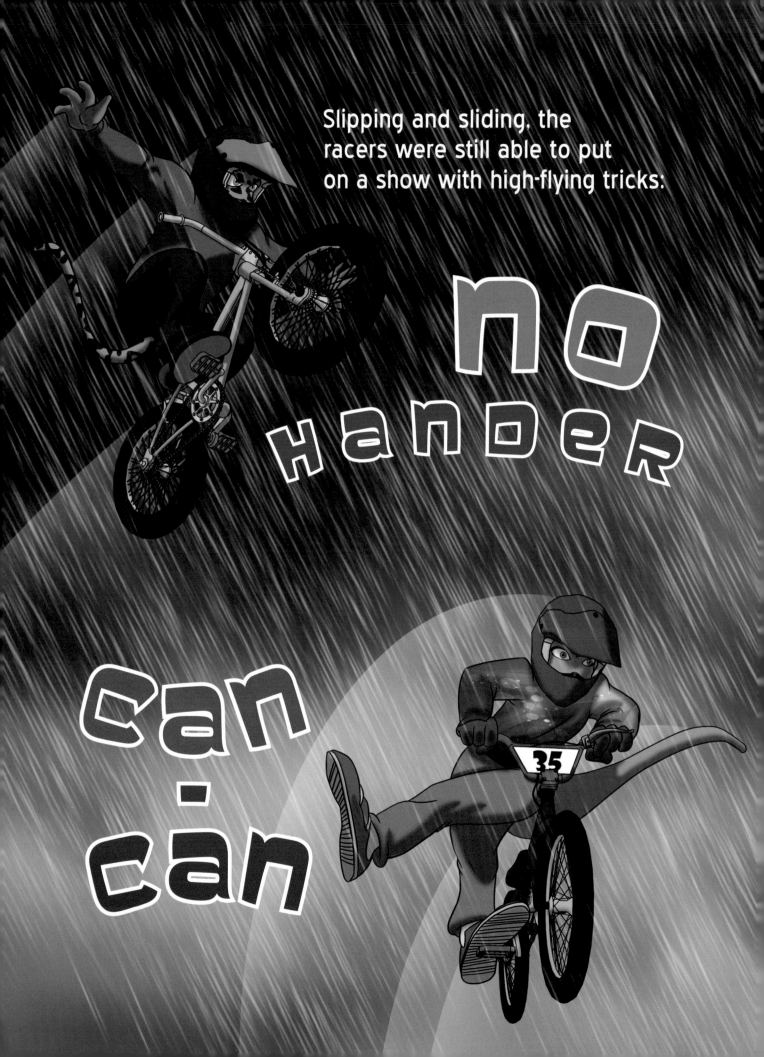

Slipping and sliding, the racers were still able to put on a show with high-flying tricks:

no HANDER

can-can

TaBLeTOP

and a

SUPERMAN

They jumped over the ooey-gooey slime, but when Mischief and the cheetah landed, their tires stuck in the mud. They flew over their handlebars and ended up with a face full of muck!

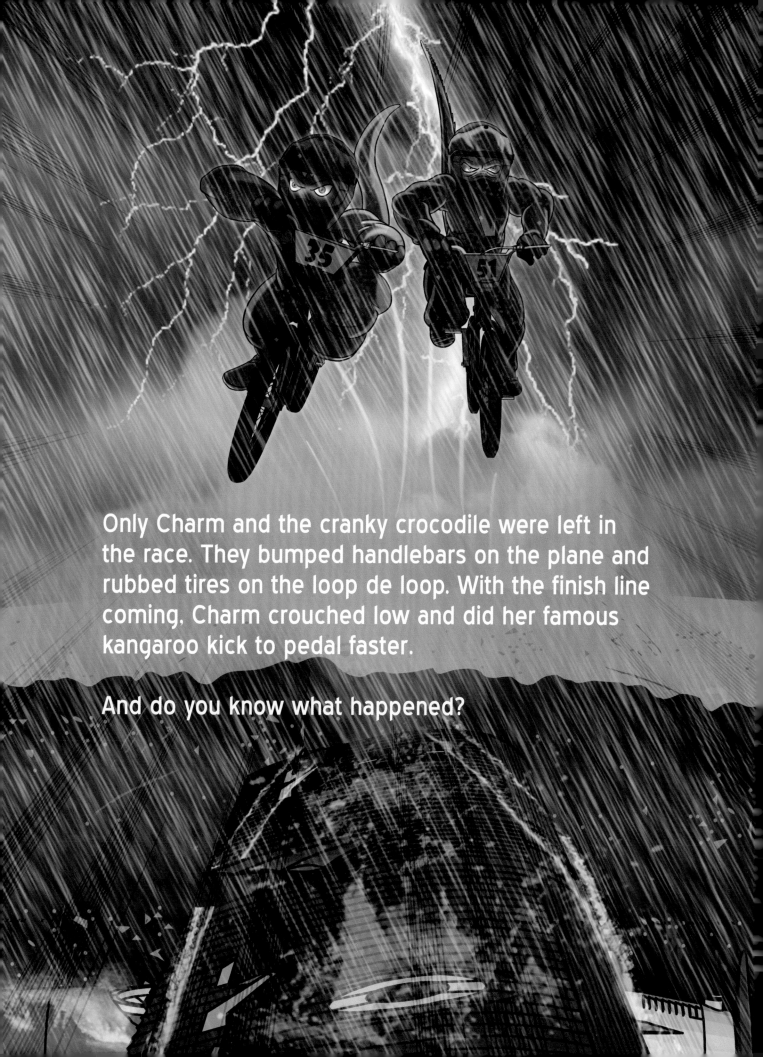

Only Charm and the cranky crocodile were left in the race. They bumped handlebars on the plane and rubbed tires on the loop de loop. With the finish line coming, Charm crouched low and did her famous kangaroo kick to pedal faster.

And do you know what happened?

She tried to go faster, but it was like pedaling in quicksand. At the last second, the crocodile popped a wheelie and lifted his front tire out of the mud. He zipped past Charm and crossed the finish line first.

The crocodile had won the

GOLDEN BIKE!

The X-tails ran up to Charm, who had a big, happy smile. "I had a blast even though I didn't win! You were right Wisdom—believing I CAN is much better than saying I CAN'T. I just had to try!"

"Wow!" said Crash. "You and Mischief are so muddy I hardly recognize you two."

Charm and Mischief looked at each other with sneaky grins and said, "This calls for a group hug."

"Not a group hug!" the other X-tails begged. But it was too late—Charm and Mischief had their muddy paws all over them. "Oh gross!" they squealed.

After lots of giggling and laughing, they congratulated
the winning crocodile, who didn't look cranky anymore!

THE TRICK-TIONARY

BUNNY HOP

This is one of the first tricks to learn. With speed, the rider jumps the bike into the air from flat ground. One common mistake is jumping both wheels into the air at the exact same time. Instead, the rider pulls up on the front wheel first and then the back wheel follows. Charm the Kangaroo has her sights set on a Bunny Hop over the X-van. Do you think she can do it?

BARSPIN

Jumping high into the air, the rider spins the handlebars one full rotation and catches them before landing. After learning this trick, go for a Double or Triple Barspin—but watch out, it might make your head spin!

Can-Can

Riding off a jump, the rider takes a foot off one of the pedals and kicks their leg over the top tube of the bike. Before landing, the rider returns their foot to the pedal. At first, try small kicks over the top tube, and when you're comfortable, go for a big kangaroo kick. After the Thunder Track race, Charm no longer says "can't"—she says "Can-Can!"

Catwalk

Sometimes called a Wheelie, this trick starts with the rider leaning back and lifting the front wheel into the air with one hard pedal stroke. The rider continues to pedal with the front wheel in the air and the back wheel on the ground. Of course, Wisdom the Lion has the Catwalk mastered!

Manual

The rider pulls up on the handlebars and rides on the back wheel. It's similar to a Catwalk except no pedaling is required for this trick. A manual helps to gain speed when racing through bumps, which is called a rhythm section. Do you know who has rhythm? Crash the Hippo, because he loves dance music!

no Hander

Soaring off a jump, the rider brings the handlebars up to their belly and squeezes the top tube between their legs. Now the scary part—the rider lets go and raises their arms high into the air. The last step is grabbing the handlebars before landing. To learn a No Hander, try starting with the easier One Hander!

Superman

Riding off a jump, the rider removes both feet from the pedals and pushes the bike in front of them. The handlebars are held with a tight grip and the rider flies through the air like Superman. Before landing, the rider returns their feet to the pedals. No superhero powers needed for this trick, just lots of practice!

TABLETOP

In the air, the rider tilts the bike to one side by turning the handlebars and using their bottom foot to pull the bike up to make it flat like the top of a table. Then the rider returns the bike to its original position for a perfect landing. Mischief can hold his bike in the Tabletop position for so long, he could have lunch up there!

TAILWHIP

Catching big air, the rider swings the bike one full rotation while holding onto the handlebars. The handlebars and rider's body stay still and only the bike frame rotates. When the bike has swung all the way around, the rider jumps back onto the pedals. It took Flight the Gorilla a long time to learn to Tailwhip, especially since he doesn't even have a tail!

THREE-SIXTY

On a medium to big jump, the rider starts the spin by turning their head and shoulders to look at the back wheel. Both the bike and rider's body spin a full rotation before landing. After learning to Three-sixty, try combining your tricks—like a Three-sixty Tailwhip!

L.A. FIELDING

L.A. Fielding is an author of children's literature and a member of the Canadian Authors Association. He dreamed up the X-tails for his two children, while telling stories on their long distance trips to the mountains each winter weekend. It is his family's cozy log home in Prince George, British Columbia, and their Fielding Shred Shack at a local ski resort, where he draws his inspiration.

Growing up skateboarding, biking, and snowboarding, L.A. Fielding now shares the fun of those sports with his family. When not writing or telling stories, he focuses his thoughts on forestry as a Registered Professional Forester. *The X-tails BMX at Thunder Track* is his fourth book in the X-tails series.

Other books in the series include:

- *The X-tails Snowboard at Shred Park*
- *The X-tails Skateboard at Monster Ramp*
- *The X-tails Ski at Spider Ridge*
- *The X-tails Surf at Shark Bay*
- *The X-tails Mountain Bike at Rattlesnake Mountain*
- *The X-tails Heli-Ski at Blue Paw Mountain*

WWW.THEXTAILS.COM